BENITO'S DREAM BOTTLE

by NAOMI SHIHAB NYE   pictures by YU CHA PAK

Simon & Schuster Books for Young Readers

SIMON & SCHUSTER BOOKS FOR YOUNG READERS
An imprint of Simon & Schuster Children's Publishing Division
1230 Avenue of the Americas
New York, NY 10020
Text copyright ©1995 by Naomi Shihab Nye
Illustrations copyright ©1995 by Yu Cha Pak
SIMON & SCHUSTER BOOKS FOR YOUNG READERS
is a trademark of Simon & Schuster.
Designed by Christy Hale
The text of this book is set in Calligraphic 810.
The illustrations are rendered in watercolor.
Manufactured in Hong Kong by
South China Printing Company (1988) Ltd.
10 9 8 7 6 5 4 3 2 1
Library of Congress Cataloging-in-Publication Data
Nye, Naomi Shihab
Benito's dream bottle / by Naomi Shihab Nye ; pictures by Yu Cha Pak.—1st ed.
p. cm.
Summary: Fearing that his grandmother has stopped dreaming,
Benito helps her to fill her "dream bottle" once more.
[1. Dreams—Fiction. 2. Grandmothers—Fiction.]
I. Pak, Yu Cha, ill. II. Title
PZ7.N976Dr 1995
[E]—dc20 93-45675
ISBN 0-02-768467-9

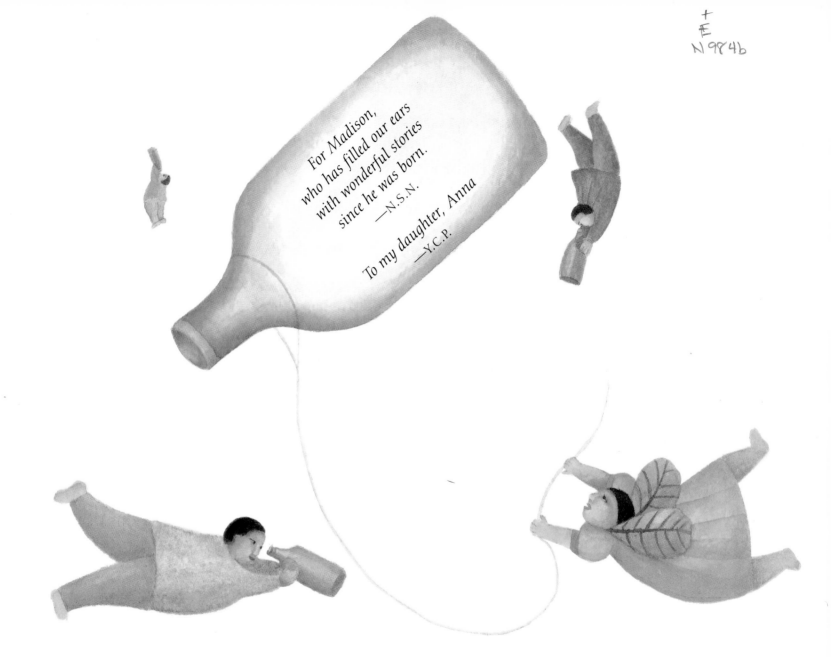

For Madison,
who has filled our ears
with wonderful stories
since he was born.
—N.S.N.

To my daughter, Anna
—Y.C.P.

At breakfast Benito asked his grandmother what she had dreamed last night, and she couldn't remember. She said she hadn't had a dream in a long time.

Benito said, "That's terrible." It sounded like a sickness. He wanted her to get well.

Where did dreams come from?
Benito asked everyone he knew.
His father said dreams were gifts delivered by angels.
His mother said, "You're my best dream."

His neighbor, Mr. Laguna, said dreams came to him from far back out of the past. Once, seventy years ago, Mr. Laguna had camped on the beach of an island. In his dreams he could still hear those singing waves.

His friend Annabelle said dreams came out of her toes and her elbows. Sometimes they pinched or tickled, like a stone in a shoe.

Benito's grandpa said
dreams grew on his fig tree and
he brought them inside the house
by picking bowls of plump figs.
At night they ripened inside his head.

His aunt the artist said
dreams were mysterious messages
sent by people we couldn't see.
His uncle the fisherman said
dreams were little fish nibbling
at our sleep.

Did cats dream?
What about trees?

Sometimes Benito's cat,
Jukebox, rolled over and shivered
without opening his eyes.
Was he dreaming of the dog
with big teeth behind the
neighbor's fence?

Benito had his own ideas. He was just asking people to find out what they thought.

Benito knew dreams really came from the Dream Bottle. "You have one and I have one," he told his mother. "It's inside every body, between the stomach and the chest. At night, when we lie down, it pours the dreams into our heads."

It would also work if you lay down to take a nap. Or if you wanted to feel dreamy for just a minute, you could close your eyes and tilt your head back.

The Dream Bottle had a little swivel cap that opened and closed by itself.

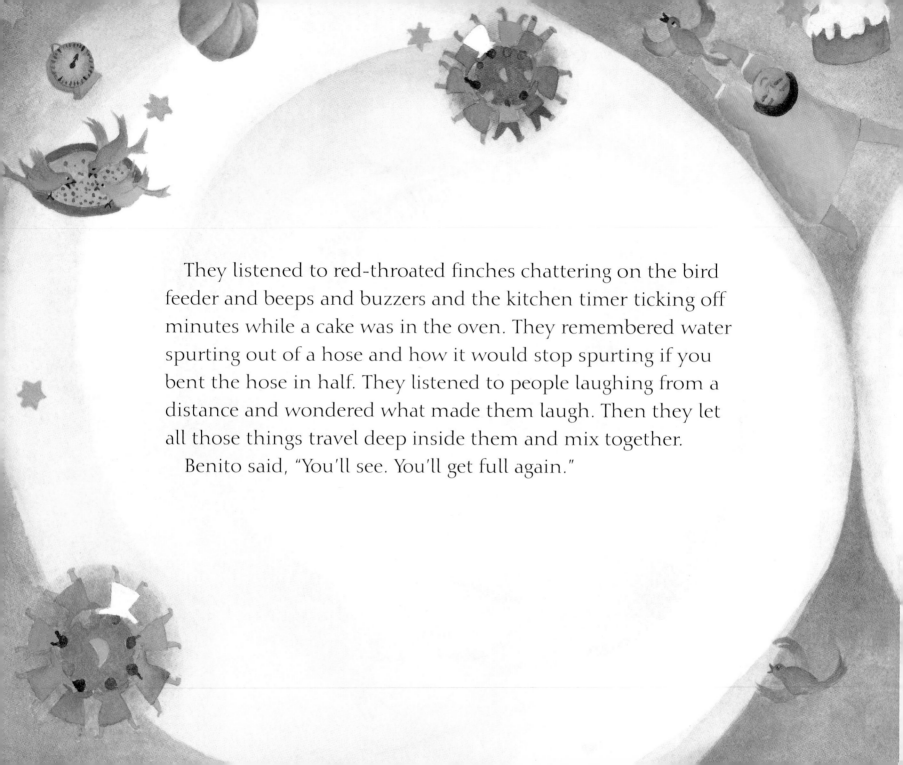

They listened to red-throated finches chattering on the bird feeder and beeps and buzzers and the kitchen timer ticking off minutes while a cake was in the oven. They remembered water spurting out of a hose and how it would stop spurting if you bent the hose in half. They listened to people laughing from a distance and wondered what made them laugh. Then they let all those things travel deep inside them and mix together.

Benito said, "You'll see. You'll get full again."

Benito took his grandmother outside to the front porch and made her sit in the swing with him. He rocked her gently side to side.

She said, "Stop. I'm getting dizzy!"

He said, "Close your eyes."

He asked, "Can you remember what a banana palm looks like with your eyes closed?"

She giggled. "Yessir! All droopy at the top—like you after you wash your hair."

He said, "What did I do when I was a baby?"

She told him he smiled and smiled and smiled.

Then he said, "What did *you* do when you were a baby?"

"I can't remember," his grandma said.

Benito said, "Tip your head back."

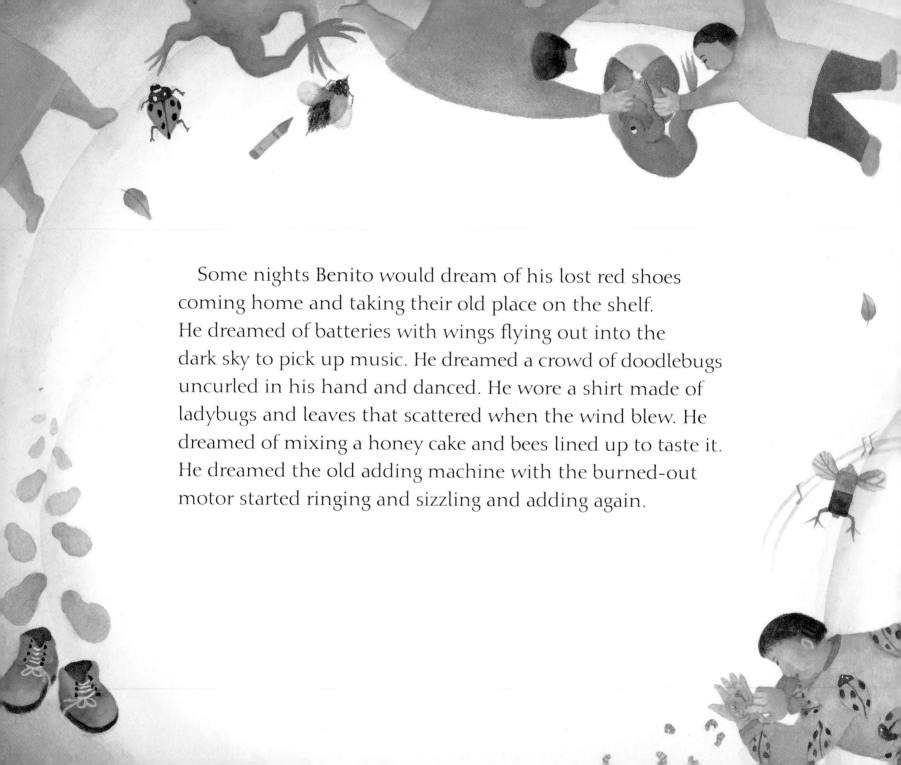

Some nights Benito would dream of his lost red shoes coming home and taking their old place on the shelf. He dreamed of batteries with wings flying out into the dark sky to pick up music. He dreamed a crowd of doodlebugs uncurled in his hand and danced. He wore a shirt made of ladybugs and leaves that scattered when the wind blew. He dreamed of mixing a honey cake and bees lined up to taste it. He dreamed the old adding machine with the burned-out motor started ringing and sizzling and adding again.

Mr. Laguna said, "Had any good dreams lately?"

Annabelle said, "You're such a dreamboat!"

His aunt the artist heard a voice come out of a pie.

His uncle the fisherman said, "Some dreams make
us patient, waiting for them."

His father said, "Have you shown Grandma the sky?
It's had pink flutters for two days now."

His grandpa said, "Don't ever stop dreaming."

At night, when his mother
bent her head to kiss him, her braid
tickled his face. Shadows from the pecan trees
made spooky moving fingers on his bed. Benito would
think of all his favorite questions: Does dust have wings? How
much does a fingernail weigh? How long does a kiss stick to a cheek?
The bottle tipped, and the dreams made pools and lakes and rivers
inside his head. He could dip his toes in—he could float and swim.

One morning his grandma told him she dreamed she
was working in the garden and she dug up a crystal button.
Also, she dreamed someone stole the legs off her bed.

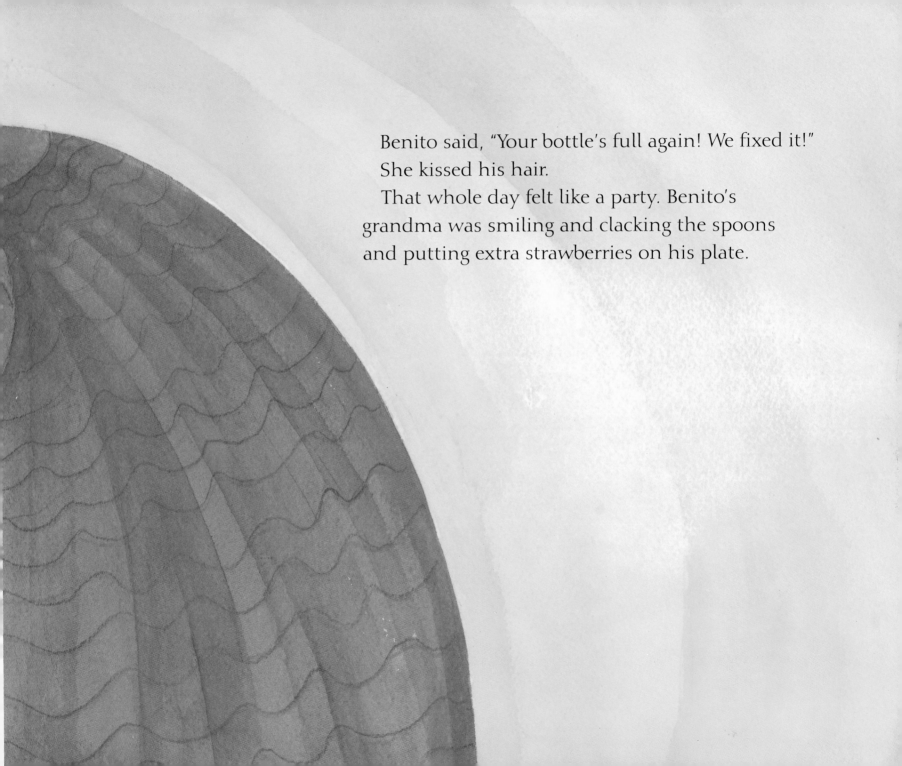

Benito said, "Your bottle's full again! We fixed it!"
She kissed his hair.
That whole day felt like a party. Benito's
grandma was smiling and clacking the spoons
and putting extra strawberries on his plate.

Later, after everyone else had gone to bed, Benito's mother and father sat in the living room, reading. When they shut their books and switched off the lights, their own dream bottles rose up again, shining. The warm blue waves carried them off to sleep.

Benito's father dreamed of cameras and Mexico
and trains.
His mother dreamed of a baby's gentle breath.
His grandfather dreamed of silver jets taking off.
Benito dreamed the letters *A* and *Z* grew so tall
he could climb on them.

And Benito's grandmother dreamed she
had a little grandson who took her by the hand
and led her outside.

He showed her how to cook leaves inside a broken
toaster oven.

He told her the yard was a hundred miles wide.